Loved by Her

The Covingtons Series

By Pixie Chica

Copyright

© 2019, Pixie Chica

Loved by Her
Cover Art by Pixie Chica

Thank You!

Thank you for your purchase Loved by Her. I hope you enjoy the story and will consider leaving a review or telling a friend about the book. I love hearing from readers! To keep in touch and follow my news, please visit me at: facebook.com/pixiechicaauthor

Loved by Her

by
Pixie Chica

Star

Nothing I've ever experienced prepared me for how I felt upon seeing her our senior year. We've been inseparable since, but to her, I'm merely her best friend while she's my world.

Seeing her with him is slowly killing me and I start to wonder if I need to let go, to accept it'll never be.

Meridien

There are expectations that come with being a Covington. I've disappointed my parents enough, I can't break their hearts, too, even when it means denying mine.

What happens when a night changes everything?

Is one woman's quest to please her family worth losing her chance at forever?

Dedication

To all those who are too afraid to come out and find love…

Whenever you're ready, the world is ready for you.

Be you, be fabulous.

Chapter One

~ Star Sinclair ~

It's not even eight in the morning and I already can't wait to get out of here. I've hated the first day of school for as long as I can remember, but this is my senior year. I'll have my diploma in a few months, which will make my parents proud. All they've ever wanted is for me to walk across that stage, something neither got the chance to do, proving everyone wrong who said they'd amount to nothing. They're both from prominent families who turned their back on them. They had to fend for themselves far too young after falling madly in love at sixteen and learning they were expecting me. The road was rough, but they gave me the best life a kid could ask for. In their eyes, I'm their biggest accomplishment, a slap in the face to all those who condemned them, and they are the only reason my ass doesn't miss a class even though I hate each minute of it with every fiber of my being.

I'm surrounded by southern belles and guys with big trucks, not that either describes everybody, but they are the majority. So, being the only out lesbian, and with numerous piercings at that, doesn't exactly earn you a lot of friends. I hang out with a couple, but they're outcasts just like me. While anyone else would've succumbed to the glances or name calling, I simply brush them off, knowing it's a reflection on them more than myself. I'm not saying that's wisdom I learned on my own, but from observing my mother over the years. She's been called a statistic and so many other things due to having me so young, yet she holds her head high, gives them a smile, then says 'bless your heart.' However, my tiny Latina mom is fiery and not ashamed of her path, so it's not unusual for her to add a 'go fuck yourself' in Spanish as she walks away, a spring in her step.

But it's a different story when my dad, a giant farmer, is at her side. Lips that would freely spew insults or gaze upon her as if she's trash seconds before when she's alone are silent and focused elsewhere, not willing to gain his wrath. She made it her mission to always make sure I knew my worth and to have thick skin when it comes to the opinions of others.

It's those lessons I hold dear as I head to my locker, one I hope won't be ransacked by idiots like mine was last year. After stuffing my books inside and closing it, I lay my forehead on the cool metal, taking a moment to shut my eyes and mentally prepare for the day. *Just get through this one, Star.* That mantra is one I'll probably repeat every morning until graduation.

I'm startled by the sound of the locker beside mine closing and silently chastise myself for not picking one further away. My theory about others avoiding those by the lab after last year's "accident" thanks to the mad scientist teacher is obviously a bust.

"Hi, I'm Meridien Covington, but you can call me Mer," a voice too chipper for this early hour says. Having no choice but to glance up, I brace myself for whatever practical joke is about to play out, yet I come face to face with a meticulously put together, southern peach. I can't stop myself from scouring the area around us, waiting for the punchline. With her fiery red hair perfectly pulled back and wrapped in ribbons and green eyes shining, she belongs on the cheer squad. Why is she talking to me?

She doesn't look familiar, I would definitely remember her if I'd seen her before, so I ask, "Are you lost?" I have this overwhelming need to protect her from how others might treat her if they see her with me. I don't give a shit what they say about me, but I see a sweetness about her that hasn't been tainted by bullies or name calling and I want her to retain it.

"Um…not particularly. My parents and I got the tour on back to school night. Dad's been traveling a lot because of his job, so we spent time in

Savannah, then a few years in Atlanta, and we just moved here. He says this is our forever home, though. Anyway, whew, that was more information than I should've shared. Are you going to tell me your name?"

She bats her eyes and I have to try really hard not to smile. She's a lot friendlier than she should be, but it's refreshing, and that means I need to nip this in the bud now.

"It's not important. You need to stay as far away from me as possible," I inform her, staring her dead in the eye.

"That wasn't very nice…" she starts to say, but I quicken my pace, leaving her behind. Complication averted, point to me. *It's for her own good.* I remind myself as I walk toward my English class and take the table in the back. I'm always early, so I put my book on it and wait for the teacher. Mrs. Smith, who I've had before, is a sweetheart and lets me come in before the bell rings. I hear the others start to pour in, their endless chatter about summer break and how spectacular everything was makes me roll my eyes as I lay my head down for a bit.

When the chair next to me scrapes against the floor, I jerk my head up, wondering who it is and come face to face with Mer, as she prefers to be called. "You're rude," she chastises me, hand on her hip with what I can only assume she thinks is a scowl aimed at me. It's almost comical actually, because she still looks cheerful. When she plops on the chair, I can feel the others staring at us.

"This seat is taken. Find another," I tell her, making sure my voice carries. Lowering it, I add, "I'm trying to help you out. Trust me." *Please let her understand.*

"Your name," she demands and I seriously start to wonder if she has a few screws loose.

"Oh good, you've met Meridien. Star, can you please show her to her next class when we're done? Her parents are dear friends of mine from college," Mrs. Smith chimes in, interrupting us, then returns to the front of the room and tells everyone to settle down. "I've got a lot to go through, but nothing too painful." She jokes.

"That's a pretty name. We'll become great friends," she predicts.

"Yay," I retort.

"Is that a defense mechanism? My brother, he's studying to be a psychiatrist, says sarcasm is an effective way to keep people at a distance." I just blink at her, having no response to that. "It's okay, you don't have to answer. He also told me people don't like to be confronted with their issues, that sometimes you have to wait until they're ready to share them with you. We'll get there, I just know it."

"Why me?" I want to know. "I'm obviously not the most conventional person here."

"Conventional is overrated, aside from that, I'm honestly not sure. You haven't run away yet, so I'll take that as a sign."

Grinning at the absurdity of it all, I remind her, "I tried, but you followed me."

She suddenly looks like she's about to burst into tears and I start to panic, checking to see if anyone is watching our exchange. They already think I'm unapproachable, this would just be proof in their eyes. "Whoa, please don't cry, I was just messing around. I'll be your friend; you seem harmless enough."

"Really?" She asks, flashing pearly white teeth at me, causing an uncomfortable ache.

"Yes, but there are limits. No trying to come to my house and stuff."

With her beautiful smile shining bright, she says, "We'll see."

Chapter Two

~ Meridien Covington ~

Six months later…

"¿Hola, Señora Sinclair, está Star en casa?" I ask, walking in without knocking, having already been told numerous times I don't need to since my first visit here. Granted, it was an unannounced one, but Star soon gave up trying to keep me at arm's length, accepting the fact it wouldn't work. The moment I saw the tall brunette with the piercings and unique style, I was drawn to her. I could see the kindness in her onyx colored eyes that she tried so hard to mask. I made it my mission to be her friend. Now we're inseparable. Her mom, Xiomara, treats me as if I were her own, feeding me whenever I'm here, so I know there are goodies waiting for me. As much as I love my parents, I have never felt as welcomed as I do here.

"I see those Spanish classes are paying off. It's always good to know a second language. Yes, mija, she is. There's some cheese pastelitos in the fridge, though I had to smack Calvin's hand from reaching for them. You know my husband is addicted to them."

"Thank you, Mrs. Sinclair. He isn't the only one," I tell her as I grab my treats. I'm not lying either, they're to die for. After a bite, you'll crave them for the rest of your life.

"My parents are visiting my brother at the university this weekend since they'll be there for a medical conference. I'm going to see if Star wants to hang out."

"You should just come here, it's not safe for a young lady to be by herself that long. And its Star's birthday, though she doesn't want anyone to know."

"OMG! How could she not tell me? Starrrrrr!!!!" I yell going upstairs. I hear her talking on the phone as I get close. I know I shouldn't listen, but I can't seem to stop.

"I haven't seen you in forever, cuzzo. I'm so fucking glad we're both eighteen now. I can't believe your parents won't let us hang out. Whatever you do…do not, I repeat *do not*, bring Mallory. I can't believe she did me like that. If all she wanted was a summer fling, she could've warned me because I'm not that kind of chick. I regret her being my first."

The thought of her being with another girl shouldn't cause this ache in the pit of my stomach, yet it does. I try to tell myself it's because I ate too many of the pastelitos, otherwise, it's due to her revelation in some way, but that can't be it.

Perhaps, having lost my own virginity to a loser, I can sympathize with Star. *Yeah, that makes sense.* It has nothing to do with the confirmation she's a lesbian, or how that word always makes me feel strange. Shaking my head to clear off these thoughts, I knock on the door.

"Come in," she says, quickly ending her call.

"Why didn't you tell me it's almost your birthday?"

She simply shrugs as if it's no big deal. "I'm just going out with my cousin, getting a tattoo, and having a small dinner with the family."

My jaw drops as if she didn't throw a bomb out there. Those are definitely not equivalent. "Whoa! Back up, back it up! I got a small dinner and a check to get a sensible and reliable car when I turned eighteen. Your parents won't kill you about the tattoo? Mine would have a coronary," I snort at my own joke, both of them being heart doctors and all, which gains me a head shake and her half-grin.

"I can legally get one without their permission, besides, you know they support me in everything I do. I'm seriously contemplating becoming a tattoo artist."

She's been telling me for months it's what she wants to do, but I didn't believe her. I've already been accepted to the University of Georgia, step one in my life plan, well, not *mine* exactly. I honestly don't want to be a doctor, but it's what's expected of me as a Covington, following the family tradition of doing so. And while I want to have kids, the road I'm taking won't exactly be ideal for raising them. My brother and I grew up without our parents around, not that they were neglectful, per se, but we were afterthoughts as their careers always came first. As a pediatrician, the children I see as patients will have to suffice. However, while I may have resigned myself to taking this path, it'll be very lonesome if I don't have Star next to me.

"My parents feel if you don't go to college, you won't get anywhere," I say with true concern. "It's what we're supposed to do."

"Mer, you know I think they're…motivated, let's call it, but it's not the only choice. Mine didn't even graduate high school. Dad makes a good living with a GED and trade school certification. I don't accept that everyone has to go, especially if they're good with their hands or have a talent they enjoy using. It'd be a waste of time."

I don't know why, but a small seed of dread hits me even though I know she's right. I'm merely being selfish in wanting her with me.

Conceding her point, I ask, "Can I go with you? Your mom said I can stay the weekend. I'd love to see one in the flesh."

She gives a hearty chuckle, saying, "Sure. If you promise you won't go crazy." I nod in agreement, not verbally doing so because I don't want to lie.

* * * *

"You sure this is safe?" I want to know, standing close as we enter the shop. Her cousin, Ricardo, has been rolling his eyes at me all day or giving me funny looks, so I'm sure my newest inquisition isn't earning me any brownie points. Thankfully, Star hasn't caught him doing it.

I've never had to be anyone but myself around her because she's always accepted me as I am, but with Ricardo here, it's as if I'm back at one of my former schools. I was viewed as too hyper and inquisitive, which meant it was hard to make friends.

"One hundred percent. A girl who works here has done a few of my piercings. Come on," Star assures me as we walk in where she's greeted by some of the guys, as is her cousin.

"'Bout time, you've been waiting on this day forever! You ready to get the skull? Jerri's anxious to do it. That drawing you two did was badass." A man who stands taller than any I've ever seen pats her on the back. His face is covered in ink, but each section is like a puzzle piece and I'm standing there mesmerized, trying to see all of it.

"It's not polite to stare, sweetheart."

Mortified, my eyes immediately move to my shoes. "Sorry, I shouldn't have done that. I was admiring your artwork. It's so intricate."

"¿En serio, porque trajiste, a la gringa Barbie?" I hear Ricardo murmur under his breath to Star and I start to panic. That's the second time I've embarrassed her already.

"I…I'll wait for you in the car," I stammer, but her tight grip stops me from leaving.

"You're not going anywhere. I want you to be here," she reminds me, her kind gaze telling me she won't let me hide. I nod, and stay where I am as she turns to her cousin. "She knows better Spanish than we do combined, so that was rude as fuck. Maybe you should go before your mom gets a picture of where you are and who you're with."

"Are you fucking serious? You're picking her over your own family?" He asks, pissed.

"She's my best friend and I want to share this with her. If you can't respect that then you're no different than your judgmental parents."

He scoffs, giving me the dirtiest look as he walks to the door and throws out, "Fuck you and your friend," as he storms off.

"I'm sorry."

"Don't be," she informs me then turns back to the man she was talking to. "As for the piece, I sketched something last night and wanted to show you guys."

"Jerri's expecting you. She has your paperwork in there," he lets her know, pointing to a room at the end. "As for you," he starts, shifting to me with a comforting smile I reciprocate, "thanks for calling it artwork. And there's nothing wrong with admiring tattoos."

Chapter Three

~ Star ~

"You sure this is what you want?" Jerri asks, staring at me like I'm crazy. Considering how often I've been here after securing this date and the fact the original tattoo concept had been finalized months ago, her reaction is understandable. But then I drew this design last night and my plan changed.

"Very."

"Okay, let me tweak it a bit and we'll get started," Jerri says, adding, "It looks great." Then she heads out, throwing a curious glance at Mer, who hasn't stopped checking out the work which is displayed throughout the space.

"These...are gorgeous. I can see why you love it, I'm sorry I doubted you before. This would be an awesome career to have. I love art, getting lost in the stuff I create, but this… this is…wow. No other word for it."

"I told you, once you fall in love with it, nothing else will do. I'm thinking of doing my apprenticeship with Jerri. She does some amazing trash polka, as well as watercolor, which is what I want to specialize in, she's also the only one in the shop that does UV ink," I explain.

"I think you'll do great. And they seem like a nice bunch here, so I'm really happy for you. Just don't be a stranger. I can't lose my bestie," I warn, playfully bumping her shoulder.

"Of course not, we're in this together. You should get one, too, make it your big rebellious act before leaving."

"My parents would kill me."

"Not if they can't see it," Jerri chimes in when she returns. "Choose a spot where clothes will hide it. You're going to college soon, after that, it's no one's business but yours."

"I couldn't...I shouldn't."

"All right. Well, there's plenty of time to think about it, this will take a while," she concedes as she sets up her station.

Mer concentrates solely on the needle on my arm, and I realize it's the most she's been able to stay focused on one thing, and I get lost staring at the calmness that's taken over her face. She's absolutely serene in this moment instead of her usual uncontainable energy that has her going a hundred miles at once.

"All done," Jerri interrupts my wandering mind, letting me know I zoned out longer than I thought. My gaze moves to the gorgeous metal-esque world now on my arm and I smile, absolutely in love with it.

"It's beautiful," Mer pipes in, taking the words out of my mouth. The way her eyes light up as she looks at it makes the piece even better in my opinion.

"It really is," I agree. "Thank you, Jerri."

"Of course," she replies, not comfortable with compliments. "What about you?" She asks Mer. "Changed your mind yet about getting one to remember this day?"

Indecision plagues her gaze and I am ready to tell Jerri to drop it because I don't want her pressured into a situation she isn't ready for. "I don't…"

"I really want to do it. I'm worried, though. Maybe a tiny design? That's easier to hide, right?" She shifts to face me, seeking reassurance as her teeth sink into her bottom lip in worry.

"Yes, but you don't have to do this. I'm the one who wanted to come," I remind her, grabbing her hand and squeezing it.

"Can we design something together?" She asks, the shy demeanor that comes out when she's afraid of being embarrassed evident.

"I would love that." A half hour later, she stares at the creation we came up with. Mer drew the basics and I added some intricate work with Jerri finalizing the more important details. The end result is a broken compass in a field of black roses.

"You do realize it's a lot bigger than what I thought you were going to go for? For a newbie who wasn't interested until you came here, I have to double-check."

"It's gorgeous and I'm getting it on my hip. As long as I don't wear a bikini in front of my parents, no one has to know," she responds with a twinkle in her eye.

"Well, let's get started." Mer lays down as instructed, then proceeds to surprise me by not flinching once throughout the whole process. She watches with wonder and awe as Jerri inks her skin, never once complaining, not even during the parts that have been known to hurt.

Two and a half hours later, we're headed home for my family dinner. Mer is silent the entire drive, eyes not leaving her hip. "You okay over there? You're awfully quiet."

"I just can't believe I got it. I felt so at peace there. I don't know how to explain it."

"You don't need to, I felt it as well." I focus on the road, turning on the radio, soft music playing in the background. My fingers start tapping the steering wheel to the beat and before I know it, we're pulling up to my house.

"Hey, wait," she says, stopping me as I open the door of my Toyota.

"What's up?"

"Thank you for sharing your birthday with me. It's now my favorite day."

"Mine, too. Now let's get in there, otherwise, the food will get cold and we'll be in trouble with my mom for holding up dinner."

* * * *

Unable to sleep I lay awake thinking of the day. I've always had good birthdays, yet this felt different, special, and I know it's because of Mer. I'm so thankful she disregarded my attempts to push her away, not once stopping her pursuit of making us friends. When she stirs, I hold my breath, not wanting to disturb her, but she's soon flipping onto her back, our bodies now shoulder to shoulder. "You awake, Star?" I tell her I am and she says, "Yeah, I can't sleep either. It felt so freeing. I just gotta last a few months, then they'll never have to know," she states, referring to her parents.

"You won't have to worry about it much longer." When she admits that she's scared, I try to soothe her. "I know, but think of what you'll get to experience. You've talked about nothing but going and being pre-med."

"What if we go our separate ways? I've never been good at making friends because I'm awkward and talk a mile a minute. I think you're the only one who hasn't noticed it. And maybe I shouldn't point that out. You could realize it and start running," she chuckles but there's sadness in it.

"Mer, we'll be friends forever. I'll only be a phone call away, even while you're on campus and I'm at the shop. Okay?" We both shift, so we're facing each other, and her eyes once more amaze me. They're such a bright green, despite the dimly lit room

"Promise?" She asks, her voice pleading, vulnerable.

"I promise. Whenever you need me, pick up the phone and I'm there."

"I'll hold you to it," she vows, pulling my arm close and laying her head on it. She falls into a deep sleep within seconds while I simply stare at her until sunrise, taking in her soft breathing and peaceful expression. *I'll always be here, no matter what.*

Chapter Four

~ *Star* ~

Three years later…

"Yo, Star, you need to answer your phone," Hansen hollers. It must be going crazy if he's interrupting me watching Jerri complete this piece. I've been working solo for a year now, but I didn't want to miss sitting in on this client. Jerri looks up long enough to nod, and I excuse myself, rush to my cell that I'd set on vibrate, which it's currently doing, making it skate across the surface where I'd left it.

"I swear to God, I'm going to kill whoever this is," I vow, pissed until I see the name on the screen. "Mer, is everything okay?" I ask as I answer, wincing at the insanely loud music blaring from the other end.

"Didn'tknowelsetocall," she slurs, something that's become quite common since she turned twenty-one. I tried talking to her about it, but she laughs it off, claiming I'm too serious. All she does now is party on the weekends, the douche her parents set her up with last month by her side. He's studying to be a criminal defense lawyer which I can't help but find ironic with how close he's been to getting a DUI a couple times. Of course, being who he is, he gets a slap on the wrist and driven home instead of arrested due to his family name. Mentally translating, she called because she knows I'll take care of her. Assuring her it's okay, I frantically ask where she is, needing to get to her before something happens. "Don'tknowNeedyou," she admits, then the sound of her throwing up follows as the line goes dead. Quickly opening the *Find my iPhone* app, thankful I had the forethought to do this where she's concerned, I locate her at yet another frat party. Unfortunately, with the late hour and traffic, I'm at least thirty minutes away. *Please let her be safe.*

After explaining the situation to Hansen and receiving a chin lift in return, I rush to my car, heart in my throat and hands shaking as I try to unlock the door. I've seen her drunk in the past, but never like this, pleading for help while throwing up. She's at her boyfriend's frat house, a place I'd prefer she stay away from as there have been some serious accusations against them lately. I continually redial her on the way, but she doesn't pick up. Running up the stairs into the house, hives starting to cover me due to worry, I start yelling her name as I walk by people in various stages of intoxication. *What the fuck have you gotten yourself into, Mer?* I think to myself as I see a half-naked couple on the couch doing a lot more than just making out. Grabbing the first idiot that looks somewhat coherent by the collar, I inform him, "Have you seen Max's girlfriend, Meridien? She has red hair and dark green eyes."

"Hey!" He exclaims, not liking my treatment of him, like I give a shit. "She's around, puking all over the place, too."

"Where's Maxwell?" I ask, thinking he might know where she is.

"He was with a brunette last I saw him," he adds, taking a sip from the cup he's holding.

Disgusted, I let him go and return to my search, finally seeing a flash of red from the corner of my eye. Jetting after her, I open the bathroom door and find her hunched over the toilet, almost covered in vomit. *Fuck.*

"Star?"

"It's me, sweetie. Let's get you home."

"I don't feel good," she states, as if that's not already obvious. With her slumped against me, my arm around her waist to hold her somewhat upright, I lead us to the door. Unfortunately, before we can get outside, Maxwell Linus Beauregard III steps in front of us. I want to throat punch him on a regular basis, but more so tonight. He's got a brunette hanging on his arm, as if he's not Mer's boyfriend. Despite the company she keeps, the chick is smart enough to make an exit. Max, the asshole that *he* is, watches as she leaves. Eyes glued to her ass the entire time. Mer, a priceless treasure, is his, yet he treats her like this?

"What are you doing here? And where are you taking my girl? I told you to stay away from her. I don't get why she's still friends with you."

"She's obviously sick and needs help, not that you'd know since you're too busy fucking other women. Now step the fuck aside before I video call her parents. If I see you doing this shit again, I'll kick your motherfucking ass. You don't scare me, pretty boy." Then, with perfect timing, my poor angel hurls, causing Max to jump back.

"Fuck! Get her out of here. She's disgusting." The urge to kill rises, but I have to remember Mer is what's important. *Always.* Easing her into my passenger seat, I take in her dirty face and disheveled appearance as I buckle her in, wondering where her joyful spirit and awe of everything around her went. An hour later, we reach the apartment I share with Jerri and her boyfriend, Tod.

Not wanting to risk her throwing up again, I gently help her upstairs and to my room, easing her into a chair. She's a lot smaller than me, which is saying a lot since I'm pretty lean, but my clothes should fit, regardless. Anything is better than what she's currently wearing. I stop by the bathroom grabbing a basin with warm water and a of couple towels.

"Let's get you clean," I suggest, pulling her shirt over her head, I throw it in my hamper before taking the wet towel from the basin of water I filled in the bathroom. She'll want, *need,* a shower in the morning, but this will work for now. Once I've wiped her face and any remnants from her overindulgence off, her eyes start to flutter open as she whispers my name.

"It's me and you're at my place. How about we get you into some fresh clothes, so you can lay down?"

"Okay," she agrees without hesitation, and the pain in my chest that's been occurring more frequently when she's in distress hits me again. I know it's tied to my urge to protect her, to keep her safe so no one can harm her. Covering Mer after she's climbed onto the mattress, her arms snake around me and she says, "You're my knight in shining armor," then places a small kiss on my cheek. The sweetness of the action has me swallowing hard, the *if only* that wants to burst from me stealing my ability to respond appropriately for a second.

Wrangling my dreams of what could be under control, I tell her, "Get some rest." Mer nods, her hands dropping to her sides as she immediately drifts off. Sitting in the chair she just vacated, I watch her sleep, not wanting to be too far, just in case. Whether she wants to or not, the two of us are having a much-needed discussion in the morning.

Chapter Five

~ Meridien ~

My skull is pounding as if it has a jackhammer in it. Sitting up, hands to my head to try and relieve the pain, I take in my surroundings and immediately know I'm at Star's. It's always nice and toasty in here, like I'm at home. I vaguely remember calling her last night, but that's it.

I was upset from what my advisor had told me, yet I don't think I drank that much, though I do remember one of Max's frat brothers handing me a drink he referred to as extra loaded. In hindsight, I can see now that's when the room had started to spin. Why hadn't I just contacted Star in the first place and shared what I'd found out? Then I wouldn't have gone to the party and gotten wasted. "Shit!" I exclaim as my brain slowly comes back online. Last night was the special client. "I'm such a fuck up."

"No, you *got* fucked up," I hear Star correct me, and follow the sound of her voice to find her sprawled out, hand covering her eyes, legs crossed at the ankles.

"I was being stupid and ruined your thing because of it. I'm so sorry!" I add in shame, tears threatening. *I'm such a fucking mess.*

"I'm glad you called me, okay? Had you not, I'm scared to think about what could've happened to you."

"My parents are going to kill me. I'm failing my classes and they're sending a letter to tell them," I blurt out all at once, needing to tell someone I know won't judge me.

"Why didn't you tell me sooner, Mer?" She asks, rushing to me and locking her arms around me. My head drops to her shoulder as her fingers run through my hair, the action so sweet it stirs thoughts I've been having recently when I'm with her. *She's your best friend, of course she cares about you. That's all this is.* Even reminding myself of that, yet again, doesn't stop them.

"I knew it was a big day for you and didn't want to bother you."

"That's not important, Mer, *you* are. I told you I am *always* a phone call away, no matter what and I meant it."

"I knew you'd drop everything and I didn't want you to. I have to forge my own path. I can't continue interrupting your life, expecting you to rescue me. I've already ruined so many things for you."

"Stop! You know that's not true," she admonishes me, placing a soft kiss on my hair. "We're going to your parents and facing this head on, which means you'll be honest about everything. If we need to call Clifton to run interference we will, but you are done being afraid of what they think of you."

"I can't do that! You know how they are. I'll have to hear how disappointed they are in me. It'll be my tattoo all over again. I can't face them. I won't," I declare, hysterically. They've grown increasingly more agitated with me and the decisions I've made. It's the reason I agreed to date Max when they introduced us as it seemed it was the only thing I could do right.

"You can and will. They'll probably be upset, but you can't keep lying to yourself to make them happy. After we leave there, we'll visit my parents. They haven't seen you in almost six months, so be ready for a big feast when I tell them you're coming over."

Her parents have always been so wonderful, it almost makes me want to do this just so I have an excuse to see them, not that I really need one. "What do I even say? Admit they wasted their money on a fuck up?"

"How about the truth? I will tell you this, you need to stop drinking now. Real life is rapidly approaching and you need to face it. I'll take you to breakfast and we'll figure this out. They'll still be upset, but if you have a plan for what you want to do with your life, you'll be able to tell them that, beat them to the next punch. I know how big they are on plans," Star tells me, her voice gentle but firm, her eyes rolling on the last sentence.

"As long as you're there, I'll do it."

* * * *

"Ready?" Star asks to my left, my hand clasped in hers, Clifton to my right. My brother was on board the moment I told him what I was doing, simply saying it took me long enough. Despite the big age difference between us, we've always been close. He actually wants to be a psychiatrist and is currently finishing his residency.

"As much as I can be," I reply honestly.

"Star and I are here," Clifton assures me, "and I'll steal their attention when I tell them I got the job at the clinic which is when you make a quick exit. I wish I could go with you, honestly, but I've delayed this for as long as I could." He knocks even though this is our childhood home, neither of us comfortable with just walking in, which is quite telling regarding our relationship with the people that gave us life. When my mother opens the door, surprise crosses her face at seeing us, but she steps back to let us in, her gaze drifting to Star with a less than welcoming expression that pisses me off. She's never liked her and would always comment that she's a bad influence when we first started hanging out.

Moving to the living room, my dad is in his favorite chair reading the newspaper, never faltering from his routine. He's a traditionalist in all ways, his words not mine, and loves the feel of it in his hands, the sound the pages make as he turns them. His life has been mapped out from an early age and he expected the same of us, so this will not be an easy conversation. He's bound to have some choice words about me quitting college, more so when I tell him the path I've chosen instead. "Meridien, Clifton," he says in greeting, adding, "and...Star. What brings you here?" It's clear he's barely paying attention even as he talks to us, too busy reading about the things going on in the world and not what's happening in his own family.

"I need to talk to you and mom. It's about school."

This has him moving faster than I've ever seen him do anything. My mother is standing next to him, both staring at me expectantly. "Proceed," he states and I start to tremble, the words I need to tell them now suffocating me. It's only a matter of time before they find out and it might be better coming from me.

Star and Clifton setting a hand on each shoulder gives me the strength to blurt, "I'm failing and withdrew from classes yesterday." Their expressions instantly morph into wrath and dad throws his beloved paper on the floor.

"You what? Are you fucking insane?" He hollers, cursing at me for the first time in my life, causing me to take a step back in fear, Clifton shields me and Star pulls me into her.

"Don't yell at her like that, Dad. She was scared to talk to you because she thought you'd be disappointed she doesn't want to be a doctor," my brother defends.

"Disappointed doesn't begin to explain what I am," Dad says.

Mom tries in a somewhat gentler tone, "Our family is full of doctors. You want to break that tradition after all these years?" As one, all gazes turn toward me, awaiting my answer.

"I've already set things in motion to become a tattoo artist."

"It's because of her! You're ruining your whole life to follow your *friend* on a path of uncertainty and bad choices. What does Maxwell think of all this? Do you actually believe he'll want to marry a tattooed nobody?"

"Enough!" Clifton shouts, trying to stop him, but it's already too late. There's nothing that can erase the look in their eyes as they stare at me now.

"You can treat me like shit and think I'm inferior all you want, but no one speaks to Meridien that way. And whatever Maxwell thinks is none of your business, nor should it matter. If he loves her, he'll accept whatever choice she makes," Star tells them, anger vibrating through her as she takes me hand and begins leading me to the door. "Let's go, Mer. Until they can talk to you with respect, we're gone."

"Oh, I'll be speaking to Maxwell, that's for sure. He's the only part of your life that's worth anything at this point!" I hear my dad yell as we walk out. *What have I done?*

"Hey," Star says, getting my attention once when we close the door behind us.

"They're so mad at me. I should've stayed in school and kept trying. There's so much uncertainty in my life while you've always known what you wanted to be."

My stomach starts cramping and I chuck it up to everything that's happened, and when she wraps me in her arms, I lean into it. Her lips press to my forehead, and I find so much comfort in the act because she's always had a way of centering me.

"Mer, you're afraid, and that's understandable. Your path has always been planned for you with no possibility of veering from it. Once you realize you deserve to be happy, things will become clear. You love the shop, and spend your free time watching me or Jerri. I've never seen you more relaxed. That's your destiny, you just need to accept it."

Taking her hand in mine, I feel electricity course through me at the contact and decide to think about it later. "What would I do without you?"

"You'll never have to find out, Mer. Now get your butt in this car."

Chapter Six

~ Meridien ~

Three years after that...

"Meridien!" His voice is like nails on a chalkboard and I'm not sure how much longer I can deal with it or him. I needed to drop his ass years ago, but every time I gather the courage to do so, I remember the way my parents light up when they see us together. Compared to how they are when I visit by myself, the thought of losing that is hard, even when I know my heart belongs to someone else.

"What?" I snap from the passenger side of his Bugatti, or Precious, as he loves to call his car, ready to get this over with. My gaze wants to return to the Tattooed Vixen, more specifically inside to where Star is talking with Bianca. I became Star's apprentice at the old shop and we were both happy there for a while, then Jerri and Hansen left as they didn't mesh well with the new owners.

We followed soon after. Felicity's shop opened a whole new clientele and challenged us to up our game. Despite all the perks, there's one downfall, *Bianca,* and I want to throttle her as she's begun to

frequent the shop more. While I try not to get jealous about it, I rarely succeed and visions of pulling her out of the shop by her hair grow stronger.

"There's a ball for my little sister tonight, so you'll need to wear something with sleeves. Take my card," he states, eyeing my jeans and t-shirt unapprovingly. "My parents' associates will be in attendance and not everyone likes…*art work,*" he adds, not bothering to hide his disdain as he skims my tattoos.

"I can take care of myself, thank you very much." He knows damn well my family's fortune rivals his, but unlike his trust fund loving ass, I became independent when I left college.

"The mall isn't exactly the place to find a dress for this event. I know you've been slumming it with these people, but you'll need appropriate attire for this."

"Felicity owns one of the best shops in the area if not the state, and runs a great program for cancer survivors. How dare you belittle her?!" I yell, getting defensive for my friend and boss.

"If you say so, dear. However, she's still not…well, I'll leave it at that because you know how your friends are. I'll call my Aunt Mary Anne; I know she'll fit you in and work a miracle." Before I can respond to that, I'm interrupted by his phone and he dismisses me as if that's that. And to him, it is. Stepping out, I slam the door shut and smirk at his reaction to it. *Fucker.* Maxwell has never liked my tattoos or career choice, something he made quite clear when I quit pre-med. Actually, it wasn't just him that stressed how disappointed they were with me. Everyone did except the one person who's always been there for me. Star's loyalty has never faltered, not even during my crazy partying days where I was using alcohol to numb the lies that were consuming me.

Walking in, I watch as Star flinches when Bianca's hand touches her forearm. I'm prepared to forcefully remove the she-devil's grip, but my best friend beats me to it. "I've already told you if you can't keep this professional you need to find another artist. As you apparently can't listen, I'll finish this piece, but I'm done after that." And then she turns to me, her eyes pleading, and asks, "Mer, since your next appointment isn't for a while, why don't you come assist me?"

"Of course. I'll escort Ms. Wallace to the room."

Star thanks me, though the snarky blonde isn't appreciative and instead scoffs, glaring at me before stomping off on her own. *That's right, bitch, Star isn't yours. She's...mine?* I try to push the thoughts away, but I know I wish it was true. I've fallen in love with her and can never tell her. For one, ruining what we have would destroy me. While I know she's openly gay and proud of who she is, she's never mentioned dating aside from what I overheard years ago as she was talking to her cousin. And I don't see her hopping into a relationship with a straight woman.

But you're not straight, are you, Mer?

Which leads to the second reason I have to keep this to myself, otherwise, I'd have to accept a side of me that I'm not sure I have enough courage to admit to. I assumed my first time had been what it was due to being a virgin, but when Maxwell tried to be intimate, I knew something was off. It just felt wrong.

It wasn't until I caught Star undressing in the apartment we now share that I realized why. When her breasts were freed from her tank top, it turned me on. When I laid down that night, I finally was able to get myself off by thinking of her. The fantasies grew from there, as did Maxwell's insistence we take the next step. I couldn't do it, not when I wanted to be with Star. I began avoiding his touch, his hand on my skin making me feel as if

bugs were crawling on me. Of course, he noticed my new aversion to physical contact which lead to him screaming at me more than once.

"I really can't stand her," Star says once I return, wrapping her arm around my shoulders and causing me to lean against her. To her, I'm just being me, but moments like this get me through the day. I can't pinpoint exactly when I fell for her, I just know one day I woke up and knew my heart belonged to her.

"That's what friends are for," I reply, trying to remind myself that's all we are.

"Yeah, friends," she says, her tone a bit somber.

Changing the subject, I tell her, "Will you be okay with me leaving early?"

"I've closed on my own before. What is it tonight?"

"His sister's debutante ball. I can't believe he's making me go, I almost punched him in the stomach. And his constant harping on this place is pissing me off."

"I don't know why you keep dealing with his shit."

"Yes you do. If I don't, my parents will completely disown me and I already have a horrible relationship with them. It's the only thing we have left that connects us."

"Mer, what they think of you is irrelevant and you know this, and that's all I'm going to say because I don't want to fight. However, he'll eventually want more, then what will you do?"

"I don't know, but I don't want to talk about it right now either."

"Fine, let's get this done. The sooner we get rid of Bianca, the better."

* * * *

"Seriously? That was the best she could do? You look like she threw something together at the last minute. And I specifically mentioned it needing sleeves. I'll be having a long ass talk with my Aunt." I roll my eyes and grit my teeth at his diatribe. I'm wearing one of the ball gowns my mother bought me a couple years ago as I didn't have time to see Mary Anne nor did I want to. She's even more judgmental than Maxwell, which is saying a lot, and I refused to listen to her talk down to me for two hours.

"I didn't go. Some of us have to work and I was already cutting out early just to be here."

He yanks on my arm, getting in my face. "Had you kept your grades up instead of partying you wouldn't have to. The least you can do is act like you belong here and stop embarrassing me. I'm fucking done with your attitude."

"I will kick you straight in the balls if you don't fucking let go of me," I warn him.

"Keep testing my patience and I'll tell your parents what you've been up to. We both know they're the only reason you're still with me. We're each getting something out of this, you want them to love you and I want their connections."

"You repulse me!"

"The feeling is mutual. Why do you think I gave up trying to fuck you? You're disgusting with all that shit on you. Be an obedient woman for once and stop your shit!" He hurls at me, tightening his grip on my arm to a punishing degree. I know there'll be a mark to remember this by and fury burns through me at that and the audacity of him to treat me like this. As we get to the center of the banquet hall where the event is being held, I lose it.

"What the fuck is wrong with you?" I snap at him.

His eyes look ready to pop out of their sockets and his smile, while appearing polite, is far from it as

evidenced by the icy daggers his eyes are aiming at me. He's livid and I truly believe he wouldn't hesitate to murder me on the spot if he thought he could get away with it.

"Have you been drinking again?" He announces when others start noticing.

I shake my head, unbelieving that he's stooping so low as to bring up something I haven't done in three years. I refuse to touch alcohol to this day because it reminds me of the mess I used to be. He finally drops my arm, taking a step away from me.

"There's not a drop of liquor in my system and you know that. I'm not like you, needing a crutch to carry me through my meaningless life. And the next time you attempt to talk to me or put your hands on me in anger, I'll make you regret it," I vow, grabbing a glass of champagne from one of the waiters blatantly listening to our conversation and throwing it in his face.

"You bitch! Get the fuck out of here!"

"Gladly!" I shout, feeling lighter than I ever have in my life as I make my exit. It's raining when I make it outside, not even caring that I can't see two inches in front of me. I'm maybe five miles from the shop, thankful they chose a centralized location as opposed to the countryside as I begin walking. With each step my mind settles and I'm at peace with the

realization I'm done. I'm still afraid of my parents' reaction when they learn of my decision, but it was eating me alive and I couldn't stand another second.

Chapter Seven

~ Star ~

This has been the day from hell starting this morning when Mer walked out of her room in bottoms so short her ass was peeking out of them and a top that barely concealed her breasts. I wanted to lay her on our table and show her how good I could make her feel, instead I took a cold shower. Add in dealing with the intolerable Bianca who better stop harassing me and the fact the one woman I can't get out of my head is dating a man who should've never been born. Talk about a shitstorm of grand proportions.

It's getting harder to be the supportive bestie because this unhealthy need to be everything for her is all consuming, even knowing it'll never be reciprocated. While I enjoy working for Felicity who is as real as they come, I've put my life on hold because I refuse to leave Mer behind. Jerri and Hansen opened a shop in L.A. and invited me to join them, but I couldn't.

When I declined, Jerri wasn't amused. She thinks my crush has run its course and I should just get laid to get over it. I know she's right about the fact I'm letting a great opportunity pass me by, but the heart wants what it wants, and mine is too stupid to understand it won't ever get it. I also know I've become the biggest cliché...falling for the straight girl.

To make matters worse, it's not as if she and Maxwell have this epic love story. He's the biggest asshole in the world and she's only with him because her parents are forcing her. They haven't actually said so, but it's obvious their "love" for her hinges on it.

Just as I finish wiping everything down, I hear someone pounding on the front door. *Who the fuck is here almost an hour after closing?* Making my way to the front, ready to scream at whoever is responsible for the racket, I start running when I can finally see who it is.

There, on the other side, is Meridien, makeup ruined, soaking wet, and red eyed. My soul wants to shatter seeing her this way. She runs into my arms and presses her lips to mine the second I unlock the door. Shocked at the action, and fearing this is all a dream, I take a step back, mouth tingling from the kiss.

"I shouldn't have done that, it's just… now that I broke it off with Maxwell, I came here hoping" she says pausing. I block the slither of hope that wants to inch its way in. There's no way she's saying what I think she's saying.

"I'm sorry, Star, please don't stop being my friend. But I've been in love with you for so long, and I want to be with you." As soon as her words register, I yank her to me. Our faces are a mere inch apart, the warmth of her breath a welcoming feeling.

"Shut up, Mer. I've fucking loved you for years. I can't remember a time when I didn't." I ravish her, our tongues dancing together, neither of us wanting it to end. It's as if we know once we do, we'll have to figure this all out. I push that thought away and just savor this moment, gripping her hair and angling her head where I want it. We don't stop until the need for oxygen demands it. Pressing my forehead to hers, I wait until our breaths are somewhat even.

"I never knew it was supposed to feel like that," she tells me and I want to kiss her all over again simply to give her more pleasure. When I hear her sniffle, I look down and see a tear rolling down her cheek.

"Fuck, don't cry," I implore, kissing it away.

"I thought it was my fault I felt sick whenever he tried to kiss me, but it wasn't that at all. It's simply because he wasn't you."

Giving her a quick kiss, still unable to believe this is real, I confess, "I couldn't date after meeting you, then I finally realized why."

"You've really loved me for years?" She asks, blinking back the rest of her tears as she recalls what I admitted earlier.

"It took me a while to accept because you were my best friend. I've always thought you were beautiful, but you were also my partner in crime."

Staring at me with her emotion-filled eyes, she wants to know, "When did you know you'd fallen for me?"

"Senior year. Carl stood you up for prom and I thought you'd be heartbroken, but you weren't, not even a little. We spent the night dancing, and we didn't leave the floor until the dance ended. That's when it clicked. I needed to keep that smile on your face forever because you were my one. To make your dreams come true."

She gasps at my answer. "You've been waiting for me this whole time?"

"I'd wait forever and a day. You know my tattoo that you love so much? The first one I got that I always keep hidden." She nods, waiting for me to continue. Gabbing the black light off one of the stations, I turn it on. "See that line in UV ink? It's the Prime Meridien, and though I knew no one would understand it, I always would. It signifies how much you meant to me then and still do."

Chapter Eight

~ Meridien ~

"What? How did I not…?"

"It's not like I made it easy." All the revelations from the last few minutes have me on edge and this feeling of need takes over. The way she's staring at me has my whole-body quivering and I can't contain myself anymore, so I close the distance between us and pull her into my arms. How could I have been so blind? Every fantasy that's played in my head pales in comparison to actually holding her, knowing she feels the same. When our lips touch, I don't even try to stop the moan that escapes at what is surely a holy moment that I never want to forget. Her softness mixing with my own is so…right, as is her groan that sends me to another level of ecstasy. Her tongue explores my mouth as mine does the same to hers. She tastes like heaven – chocolate, caramel, and decadence. Snaking my hand up her stomach, my fingers graze her breast and her nipple pebbles at the touch.

"What are you doing?" She asks, breaking contact, her face reflecting desire.

"Please," I beg, the ache almost too much to

bear. "I need to know what it's like to be loved by you. I don't want to think about anything else, just be you and me. *Us.*" If she denies me, I'm not sure I'll survive.

"Fuck! Do you know how long I've yearned for you to say those words?" She wants to know, dropping a quick kiss on me as her fingers make quick work of my buttons. When my dress falls to the floor, I'm so thankful there was nothing holding it up other than my braless breasts as I stand there in only my lace panties.

"You're a vision, baby," she whispers, making me feel beautiful, desired. "I'm trying not to lose control here."

"Lose it," I urge her, stepping out of the material pooled at my feet and walking toward her tattoo room. Hopping on the area for clients, I lay down, suddenly more brazen than I've ever been, which seems to snap her out of her stupor and into action as she follows me.

"Make no mistake," she begins, continuing with, "we aren't leaving until I've had my fill of every inch of you."

"Stop talking and fuck me," I demand, my body heated and wanting relief.

"On it," she replies, then climbs over me.

When her hot mouth lands on my breast and her palm kneads the other, I whimper from the pleasure. Star sucks on my nipple, her tongue twirling around it and I run my hands through her hair, pushing her forward to take it deeper. As good as this feels, it's not enough. I'm beyond aroused and need relief. Her hand travels down until I feel her cup my mound, when her digit pushes through my folds, I lift up unable to control my actions. Wanting to do the same for her I caress her jean covered center, fueling my desire, and need to get into her sweet spot.

"Patience, baby."

"I don't know if I can wait," I inform her, being honest. I undo her jean's button, and unzip her, my hand sliding through her panties until I can feel her wetness, and she's equally aroused as I am. Minutes pass each indulging in the first feels of each other. Our movements quicken the pace matching our urgency for more. When she flicks at my clit my back arches into her, my need to scream her name overpowering me, deafening all other sounds. I mimic her motions, causing her to shake above me with her own release, and it's as if I've conquered the world in this second. Star in the throes of passion is a sight I'll never forget.

"That was...I have no words. But I need more." I say between ragged breaths.

"So eager. Let me show you just how good I can make you feel." Next thing I know, I'm scooting toward the edge, my ass about hanging off, and she's sitting in her chair staring at my center with my legs over her shoulder. Despite having dreamed of her doing this exact thing to me, I'm nervous as hell. But like always, she knows what I need, knows the right thing to say. "I've got you," then she kisses my inner thigh and goosebumps cover my skin in anticipation. Soon I'm begging, each touch driving me a bit madder until I'm writhing with need.

"Please what? Words, Mer." She's so close to where I want her to touch that I can feel the warmth from her breath on it.

"You know what I need." My cheeks burn from embarrassment, my earlier brazenness gone now that she's asking out loud.

"Say the words and I'll make it good for you, baby," she promises, a soft kiss making contact with my core and I come undone, all hesitation instantly fading.

"Fuck me. Lick me. Take me, dammit." I'm rewarded for my bravery as she flicks my clit. Gripping the sides, I feel like I'm about to fly off the ink bed. The second I think I might be able to draw air into my lungs, her tongue dips inside and she mimics how she was fucking me with her fingers earlier. I'm no longer able to put thoughts together.

The euphoria that crashes into me is a continuous wave of pleasure that I'll never be able to describe in accurate detail. I vaguely register her hands on my hips as she pulls me closer so I'm practically face fucking her.

I lose count of the number of orgasms she's given me, yet when her lips surround my now sensitive bundle of nerves an instant before she sucks on it, a guttural cry erupts from deep within me. When I try to move, unable to take more, Star growls against my heat, "No, you're mine! That means your body and your pleasure." That's the last thing I remember.

"What the hell happened?" I ask, mortified at the realization I blacked out in the middle of my first time with Star. "And how did I get here?"

"I wrapped you in the emergency blanket you swore I'd never use and helped you to the car. You came to for a few minutes and I brought you home," she explains, softly kissing my lips and I moan when I taste myself on her.

"Stop that or you'll spend the remainder of the night sitting on my face. Neither of us will get any rest if that happens."

"Isn't the saying 'no rest for the wicked'?" I barely finish my sentence, when my still naked body is above her face, my knees on either side of her head.

"Let me have that sugar," she demands and I obey without hesitation. Why does it feel so different in this position?

"That's it, ride my face. I want your sweet juice all over it. Can you do that, baby?"

Looking down at her, seeing how fucking bad she wants me, realizing I'm in control when we're like this, I turn into a seductress. "Beg me for it," I tell her, rising so her mouth and tongue can no longer reach me.

"Every fucking moment of my life just for a drop. Please, Meridien, I need it."

"That's so unfair," I scold as I drop back down, fully aware she knows what her words did to me. I writhe on her, and when she senses I'm almost there, her hands hold me in place as she continues until I orgasm. Yawning, we lay side by side, her arms holding me tightly as if she's scared I'll disappear, I let her know, "After this nap, I want to taste you, too."

"We have all the time in the world to explore each other," she assures me in a confident whisper against my temple.

* * * *

A couple days later, we're opening as Shaynah's not due for an hour and Felicity has an appointment. We're currently in Star's room making out like teenagers but making sure not to go too far, as we did before. We replaced the bed that following morning for sanitary reasons, though Star said it was because it had my scent, and no one was going near it. I rolled my eyes at her possessiveness, but I'd be lying if I pretended it didn't make me happy. That bed is now in our apartment and the things we've done on it since makes me blush.

"We have to set up before Shaynah gets here," I remind her, stopping our kiss.

"One more," she pleads and I eagerly give in. I'm just as needy and the times we have to keep our distance are hellish until we get home. I asked her to keep us quiet for the time being, and while she wasn't thrilled about the idea, preferring to shout it from the rooftops, she agreed. I haven't even told my parents I left Maxwell.

We're lost in each other when I hear Shaynah, and I jump off Star so fast I smack into the wall as I attempt to straighten my dress.

"You good in here?" Shaynah asks, poking her head in.

"Yep, totally, nothing happening here. Why?" I'm talking a mile a minute, aware that I'm acting guilty as hell.

"All righty then," she responds, then turns to Star and says, "Whatever she's on, keep it away from me. I'm manning the phones today," she throws out over her shoulder, mumbling, "We need a damn receptionist."

"That was close." Star doesn't respond, and when I glance at her, I don't miss the tick in her jaw as she begins checking her supplies. When I touch her back, she flinches so slightly I wouldn't have noticed if I hadn't been watching her so intently.

"What's the matter?"

"You'd rather let her think you're on drugs than know we're a couple."

"No, it's not that. It's…"

Chapter Nine

~ Star ~

Slamming my hands on the wall, heart hurting, I inform her, "I'm done being your dirty secret. I thought I could do it; I've had practice hiding what I feel for you for so many years. You were the impossible dream, something I could never have, but now that I have you, I want everybody to know."

"You know how people will react, especially my parents, when they find out. I can't take the way they look at me when I disappoint them."

"That's just it, Mer. You stayed in a loveless relationship, hating everything about yourself to the point you were physically ill to keep them happy, and they never once saw how it made you feel. Maxwell also treated you like shit for three years and you put up with it because you think they'll love you! I *do* and you want to hide that! That's not fair to me." Needing to get away, I push through the door and stumble into Felicity.

"What the hell?"

"Shit, I'm sorry. I didn't see you there. I just

need some air."

"Sure you do. This have anything to do with Meridien?"

"Why would you think that?"

A brow raises and her hand goes to her waist, letting me know I'm in for it. "I'm not stupid. You've been attached at the hip as long as I've known you, but now there's this tension that wasn't there before. I have a few minutes. Let's grab a cup and talk." We head to the diner down the street that has the best southern comfort cooking I've ever had, and she doesn't waste a second to demand, "Spill it," after the waiter takes our order. "What's going on? And don't lie to me, you know I'm like a vault. Whatever is said between us stays that way."

The need to talk to someone wins, that and the fact I can trust her. "Meridien and I are in love," I inform her, waiting to gauge her reaction before continuing.

"No shit. It's about time. Now keep going because I know that isn't all of it."

"She doesn't want to tell her parents, nor anyone for that matter, and I'm not sure I can live in the closet again. But I also don't want to lose her." She's quiet as our food is delivered, thinking about my problem, so I wait, not knowing what else to do.

Felicity grabs my hand and squeezes it. "You've known who you are since you were a teenager. You've waited for her for years. We both know Meridien has struggled with so much because of her family, yet she took a huge leap in accepting and acknowledging how she feels about you. I'm not saying your feelings aren't valid, but I want you to look at it from her side, too. And ask yourself this – is she worth it? If the answer is yes, then you know what to do."

"She's worth everything." Felicity smiles at me, though there's a bit of sadness reflected in it, and I wonder if it has to do with Parker. I know she loves him, but she seems to fight him the majority of the time. My mind made up, I ask for and am given a few hours to get my thoughts in order and figure out how to make things right. I head to my parents, needing my mom and walk in, calling out, "Ma, I'm home."

"There's my baby!" She exclaims, kissing my cheeks and giving me a big hug. I've missed her so much, even though it's only been a few weeks since I was last here. "Where's Meridien?"

"At the shop. She's actually why I wanted to talk to you."

Worry crosses her features, and she immediately wants to know, "Is she okay? Did that douche do something to her? I don't know when that girl will realize she needs to dump his ass."

"She did, but I'm not sure if who she's dating now is any better."

"She's already dating someone else? She was here less than a month ago, how much could I have missed? Next you're going to tell me you have a girl."

"I do." Her mouth drops open and she acts hurt. I simply roll my eyes at her, letting her pull me into the kitchen where she grabs us coffee and one of her famous desserts. I'm full from lunch, but I don't dare refuse. I make a mental note to take some home for Mer, I might need the brownie points. "Well, Mer is dating a stubborn ass that won't let her come out on her own terms because she's too focused on wanting everyone to know Mer is hers."

Mom is in mid-gulp and sprays it on the table in shock. "She finally came out?" Should've known nothing gets past this woman. "Whoever this is, I'm going to kick her ass. Hell, why haven't you? No one can tell you when or how to come out. I'm not a proud PFLAG member for nothing." I love that she's so into the community that she became a member of the local chapter that helps parents come to terms with their kid's sexuality.

"Because I can't kick my own ass," I admit, waiting for her to catch on.

"What? Thank fuck! Otherwise, I was going to be disappointed you weren't the woman she'd fallen for. Oh god, the Covingtons will have a fit. I'll have to warn your dad they might come over and cause trouble. I'll set them straight if they try…" then she stops mid-sentence and smacks the back of my head. "Are you stupid?"

"Ouch!"

"I can't believe you tried to rush Meridien. I hope she breaks up with you to teach you a lesson. Scratch that, I need you two together or I'll lose her. Most days I like her more than I do you. Hashtag sorry not sorry."

"Did you really just say that?" I ask, mortified.

"Why are you still here?" She wants to know, ignoring my question. "Find her and grovel." Then she starts muttering under her breath, "You're as clueless as your dad."

"Hey, I came to talk to you, didn't I?"

"You came, you saw, you conquered, now get the fuck out of here. If you don't hurry, you'll never come again, if you get what I mean," she states, wagging her eyebrows in glee.

"Ewwwww! What the fuck, ma? You've been

hanging around the kids at the youth shelter a little too much. Not cool."

"Oh please, I'm the most popular volunteer there. And be warned, there will be others ready to replace you if you don't fix this with my future daughter-in-law." Her calling Mer that warms my heart. I'm truly blessed to have such supportive parents.

"Thanks for being so wonderful. Those kids are lucky to have you. I know I am." She kisses my cheek and I head back to my car, intent on making things right.

Chapter Ten

Watching her walk away for the first time in all the years we've known each other hurt like a bitch. Making my way to the front, I hope we find a receptionist that's a good fit soon because I know Shaynah hates manning the desk. When the door opens, I hope it's Star because my heart is breaking with every moment we're apart, but it's Felicity's friend.

"Hey, Vanessa. What can I do for you?" Shaynah asks as the phone rings.

"I'll take care of her," I offer a relieved Shaynah who is thankful for the help.

"Is Felicity here?"

"She should be soon. Would you like something to drink while you wait?"

"Water, please." After getting it for her, she glances at me and asks, "Are you okay? You look like you've been crying."

"That time of the month, so my emotions are

crazy," I lie. She's a sweetheart, but I don't know her like that and I'm ready to meet my brother for lunch. When I called him earlier, bawling, he invited me to lunch, knowing I needed him.

"If you say so, but just know we girls gotta stick together. I know we don't know each other that well, but I can tell when someone is in distress."

"Thank you. That's very nice of you. My brother should be here any minute though, and I think only he can help me right now." The sound of the door opening again gets my hopes up once more, though they instantly deflate when Felicity comes through. She and Vanessa stride toward her office, but not before she throws a glance at me.

"Your brother is here, but you and I will be talking later."

"Hello to you, too," he greets as I give him a tight hug as soon as he opens the door. "Everything okay, kiddo?"

"Can we go somewhere private? I don't want you to freak out when I tell you."

"You're worrying me. Are you sick?" He asks, inspecting me for any injuries. I assure him I'm not when he doesn't stop fussing over me.

"Let's go to my clinic. No one will bother us there. We'll pick up some sandwiches on the way." He keeps glancing at me during the drive, like I'm about to break some horrible news to him, and I hope he doesn't view it as such when I tell him.

He's always been very open and gets along with Star but accepting someone as gay and learning your sister is, are two different things. Once inside, I sit on the swivel chair I love so much wondering if this is the last time I'll be invited over.

"What's going on? You know I won't be able to eat anything until you tell me."

I scooch toward his desk, trying to contain my tears, I say, "I broke up with Maxwell."

"He wasn't good enough for you."

"I'm not done," I warn him, taking a deep breath. "I'm gay and madly in love with Star. Don't hate me," I blurt out, heaving as my vision blurs. I feel his arms wrap around me and lean into him.

"I could never hate you. I love you and always will." His words fill my heart with such love and hope. "I've wondered for a while but could never figure out why you two weren't more than friends."

I can't even describe the feeling of being

accepted by him. All this time I was worried of how he'd take it. I should've known I could count on him. When I finally calm down, he sits across from me and opens our sandwiches. I haven't been eating much lately and Star has been worried about me, so I try to take a few bites.

"Have you told her how you feel?" He asks, sensing there's more to the story.

"Yes, but I think I messed everything up between us."

"How?"

"She's upset because I kind of shunned away from her this morning when Shaynah almost caught us. I'm just not ready to come out to everyone yet. What if I never am?" He stares at me and I recognize the look as his 'are you kidding me?' expression.

"I can't imagine how hard this must be on you, especially where Star is concerned because she's always been unapologetically her, but you can't let the opinions of others dictate your life. You have to see that hiding how you two feel about each other is like admitting you're ashamed of her. Maybe taking some time is the best thing for you to do. You can test the waters and figure out what you really want."

"I want Star. I've waited long enough," I say, getting defensive.

He smiles at me, and I realize I fell right into his trap.

"Then what are you going to do? Even if she forgives you, this will eventually come up again. Put yourself in her shoes. If she's been in love with you for as long as I suspect she has, she's had to watch you with a man that is the scum of the earth for years. How do you think that makes her feel? Is she less worthy than him?"

"Oh my god, what have I done? She's going to hate me or even worse, fall out of love with me."

"I think you could shoot Star in the foot and she'd blame herself for standing too close. I've never seen anyone more devoted to someone than she is to you. But you need to make sure she knows you love her and to be patient, because this is all new to you."

Feeling a hundred time better about what I need to do, I hug my brother. I knew he'd be the one to help me sort through everything. When I pull back, I slip a bit and a single file falls on the ground. When I crouch to pick it up, he becomes apprehensive. Snatching the folder away from me. But not before I see a photograph of a beautiful woman about my age. It's a candid shot of her laughing at something.

"Who is that?" I ask, but he claims it's no one.

"That doesn't seem like no one to me. Is there something you want to talk about?" He wipes his hand across his face knowing I will get to the bottom of this.

"She's a patient. That's all you need to know. She's an angel that lost her way and I'm hoping I can help her." When he speaks of her, he gets the same look in his eyes that I've seen in mine when I talk about Star. *He's in love with her.*

"If anyone can help her, it's you."

"Thank you. Now let me get you back or Felicity will have my ass for making one of her artists late."

When I walk in, Star runs toward me, cupping my cheeks for a second before letting go, as if she's scared about my reaction. That more than anything is proof of how much I messed up. She should never feel like that with me.

"Sorry, I… can we talk in private?" She whispers.

"No more private talks."

Her eyes widen and I don't miss the tremor that goes through her. "Please? I know I shouldn't have pushed," she says, desperation clear in her tone.

"I refuse to make you feel this way anymore. You're everything to me and I don't care who knows it," I inform her, kissing her in front of everyone. I hear the hooting and hollering from those in the shop, my friends, my true family.

"What in God's name is happening here?" And yet my dad's voice still has the power to freeze me in my tracks.

Fucking shit. I wasn't prepared for this.

"Get your hands off my daughter!" My mother exclaims. I take one last look at Star, fear once more clouding her and I turn to my parents. They're mad, that much is obvious, but I suddenly realize I don't really care.

"I was the one kissing her."

"When Maxwell told us you broke up with him a week ago, we knew you'd finally lost your marbles and I needed to save you from this life. I always knew Star was bad news, but your mother and her soft heart made me keep quiet. Well, no more. Say goodbye and let's go. I'm calling Maxwell to start wedding plans."

"The fuck you are!" Star says stepping in front of me to guard me from their wrath, and while I love her for that, it's time I fought my own battles.

"I got this, baby. You've done enough," I inform her before turning to my parents. "I'm not leaving nor marrying anybody other than this woman as soon as I can. And you're going to stop putting my life, friends, and fiancée down. I've already told the people that matter and they're all in this room, minus my brother who knows and supports me. So either you accept it or I'm done with you."

"You don't mean that. This is not how we raised you. I'm not leaving without you and you can't force me."

"I sure as shit can!" Felicity yells. "Get the fuck out or I'll call the cops on you."

"Fine, but don't come crying to us when things go bad for you, and they will," Dad declares in a scream. My mom looks mortified at his words, though.

"But she's our daughter, she'll come to her senses," she pleads.

"I won't. I don't blame you if you go with him, just know it's mutual. I won't reach out or let you back into my life until you can accept me for who I am."

"Let's go!" My dad says, pulling my mom with him as she stares at me as if I've ruined her life. Too bad. It's time I loved myself enough to be happy.

"You okay, baby?" Star asks.

Despite what just happened, I'm finally at peace, and with the person I'm meant to spend my life with. "I got the girl; how could I not be?"

"If I haven't said it enough, I fucking love you," she says giving me a kiss.

"Keep saying it, we've got years to make up for."

Chapter Eleven

~ Meridien ~

Two months later...

In less than twenty minutes, I'll be walking down the aisle and marrying the woman I love. Not in a million years did I ever think this would be possible. We spent the night together because I didn't want to do the traditional thing, still feeling as if I was dreaming, I needed to be with her to prove to myself it was real.

Clifton joins me and places his hands on my shoulder. "You ready?" He's the only one from our family. Along with Juliana who has now become like a sister to me. Turns out he had a few secrets of his own. When my brother came clean, I couldn't believe the story of how they met.

"I'm over the moon. I know how lucky I am that she loves me. The moment that ring gets on her finger it will never come off."

"You're insane. And I mean that in the best possible way. You have control issues."

"No head shrinking. I'm just mad about my

woman and I don't care who knows it. Now take me to my wife."

"She could still back out."

"May your tongue turn to chard, you asshole. I'm going to tell Juliana not to give you any for a week."

"Wow, that's low, don't you dare tell her that. Now let's go, I'm sure Star is just as nervous as you. I can't believe you'll no longer be a Covington after today." The music starts to play and we walk hand in hand one step closer to my forever.

Star has her hair up and she's wearing a gorgeous white dress with lace that provides a beautiful contrast to her tattoos. I take my spot next to her and get lost staring at the woman who is about to become mine in all ways. I get so distracted I don't realize I've missed my cue.

"Stop staring at her boobs and seal the deal," I hear Felicity yell, which causes everyone, including myself, to laugh.

"I can't help it. Have you seen her?" I joke, then get serious and squeeze Star's hand. "When we first met, I saw a girl that wanted to run as much as I did, but I refused to let you escape. I convinced myself you'd become my friend, my only one at that. That should've been when I realized I'd be able to do anything with you by my side. You give me the courage to be myself, to choose my life and fall in love. I ask you to continue to make this life an adventure, to love me as much as I do you, and kiss me senseless every day of my life."

"Like I'd say no to that," Star responds as I place the ring on her finger. "I fucking do!"

"Mer, I thought you were crazy when you approached me because I had no idea why you picked me; however, we were made for each other. It just took us a bit to get here is all. But given the chance, I'd do it again. I love you beyond reason, in this lifetime and the next. I will always love you and be what you need, so make my soul complete and become my wife."

"Yes!"

"Thank fuck! I can finally stop chasing you," she states, kissing me in a way that is nowhere near decent, not that I give a fuck. "This ass is finally mine," she shouts to our guests as her hand squeezes said ass.

"And yours is mine."

Epilogue One

~ Star ~

Four years later...

Walking into our bedroom, my heart breaks when I see her crying. As much as I want to hold her and tell her everything will be okay, I'd be lying. We've gotten our hopes up so many times, only to be disappointed. After our ceremony, we really talked about what our future would entail and Meridien has always wanted children. I intended to make it happen, but four years and many unsuccessful tries later, including a false positive that almost tore her to pieces, it hasn't come true. After that last attempt, I was hesitant to continue trying, the pain in her eyes killing me. We made a pact that if this time didn't work, we'd wait a while.

As much as I want kids, too, I can't bear to see her go through another round of procedures. Which leads us to this moment. Wrapping an arm around her shoulders, she leans into me, and I send a silent prayer to whatever higher power is up there, not for me but for her, that this is it.

"I'm scared," she confesses, and I hold her

tighter, trying to be her rock once more.

"No matter what, we'll get through it together. Nothing will ever change that."

"I know. I just didn't think it would be this difficult." Laying a kiss on her forehead, we sit there, knowing in a few minutes we'll hope for the best. In my mind, I see an exact replica of the woman that owns my heart filling our lives with laughter, and mischief. Sometimes, after she's spent hours envisioning that child, I can almost see her come to life, too. Let this be positive.

"You ready?"

"As much as I can be." We will face the world head on. I follow her into the bathroom, fully aware peeing on the stick is the easy part, the hardest is the wait. As we prepare to do that, the phone rings.

"Hey, Clifton. What's up?" I ask, finding it weird he's calling as he's supposed to be leaving for vacation with his wife, Juliana, and their child, Zeny.

"Mom was in an accident and Dad wants us to go to the hospital. Can you come?" Shit, this is the last thing we need right now. Mer hasn't spoken to her parents in four years and I don't want to tell her, but she misses her mom.

"Shouldn't his butt be on the ramp?" She sees the look on my face and pales. "Is Zeny okay? Juliana? What's wrong?" When I tell her what's going on, she wants to know, "Why now? They made it very clear they want nothing to do with me."

I grab her hands and kiss them. "He knows you don't want to be anywhere near them, so if he's telling us to go, then we should. I'll be right next to you. I'd never let anyone hurt you."

"If this is some ploy, I'm out." We leave, the pregnancy test momentarily forgotten until we get in the car. "The quicker we leave, the sooner we get home. Whatever the result, it'll wait. We don't want to think about that while dealing with your parents."

"Fine, but I want to know what it says. So let's make it quick, I'm not keeping my hopes up on what he wants to do with me." The hospital is only a few minutes away, so it doesn't take long to get there. Her dad is in the waiting room, hands on his head, blood on his clothes. The man is in obvious distress and Mer instantly rushes to his side, back to being that young girl who loved her parents without fault, even if they weren't the nicest. "Where's Mom?"

"Meridien, I didn't think you'd come. I'd hoped, but with the way we left things…It was so stupid. Please forgive me. I've been wanting to tell you how sorry I am. And now this…" He pulls her into a hug, a deep sob leaving him. The man that never showed a sliver of emotion seems to have become undone.

"It'll all be okay, dad. I still love you and mom, but I had to be happy, too, and that meant being with Star." I make my way over to them wanting to be close in case he rejects her again.

"I know that now. I knew it the first time you defied us, and Star stood next to you. Your mom, too, she told me that night the future was inevitable. I didn't want to believe it because I couldn't see past my own wants. Star has always been there and I'm glad you found each other. I know we haven't been the most loving people, but your mom is my everything. As Juliana is to Clifton and Star to you. I'm so sorry."

"I forgive you. Star convinced me to come and I'm very glad she did." Dr. Covington looks right at me and opens his arm at that news. The last time we were at his house I was thrown out while Meridien bawled, but there comes a time you have to be the bigger person and accept that people can change. He hugs me tight and I can feel his tears on my shirt.

"Thank you for giving her the love she deserved. I'm sorry for the way I treated you," he whispers. It's hard to accept when you're wrong, even more so to apologize for it.

"Sorry to interrupt," an older gentleman in a white coat says as he joins us. "Your wife will be okay. She does have multiple broken bones and fractures, but she is in no immediate danger. She is awake and calling for you, Dr. Covington."

"Thank you so much. I need to see her." There in the bed is Meridien's mother, bloody and bruised. As expected, my wife starts to cry all over again.

"My baby. Look at you!" Her mom exclaims, grimacing when Mer squeezes too tight.

"I'm sorry, I've just missed you so much. What happened?"

"I wasn't but ten minutes from the house when this car comes out of nowhere. I faintly remember being pulled out and getting rushed here but that's it." I immediately want to know if she thinks it was a drunk driver and Mer's dad takes over from there.

"It was that bastard, Maxwell. Apparently, it wasn't the first time either. There will be no slap on the wrist or enough money to fix this. It makes me sick to think I wanted my daughter to marry him." Bile and anger shoots through me at the mention of that piece of shit.

"Are you serious?" Meridien asks, dumbfounded.

"When I got the call and ran to the scene, he was still there. I attacked him, so I'll have to go to court, but it was worth it."

"Go dad," Clifton, who has been quiet this whole time, states. We were lucky they let us back as visiting hours were almost over, but Zeny needed to get to bed, so Juliana took their daughter home and he stayed.

"I would've killed him had the cops not been on me within seconds," Dr. Covington informs us, rather proud of himself. If it had been me, I'd feel the same I think with a smirk. That idiot deserves all the punishment he has coming.

"Well, at least something good came out of this, we're a family again, which means I don't have to shrink my own family anymore," Clifton remarks, causing us to laugh. We stay a bit longer, then head home. Mer falls asleep on the way and I let her rest, knowing what's waiting for us when we get there. I wake her gently and we walk in silence to our room.

"I've gone through so many emotions in the past few hours, I'm tempted to not look."

I lift her chin and kiss her lips softly, whispering, "We have each other and a love that spanned years of adversity. It will still be us tomorrow, and the next day, until my last breath, because I will always be your knight in shining armor." Hand in hand, we check the test, reading the result at the same time. Positive. *I will always make your dreams come true.*

Epilogue Two

~ Meridien ~

Eight years after that...

I'm finishing the last of the dishes, determined to leave everything spotless before we head out. Felicity closed the shop for the week and we're all going on a Disney cruise. Star and I had a little girl, Scarlett Corazon, and while I always wanted a big family, I knew I couldn't go through that process again.

When Scarlett was twelve months, we adopted our second daughter, five-year-old Summer Lynn. Appearance wise, they are complete opposites as Scarlett inherited my red hair and green eyes, while Summer has black hair and brown eyes. She could've easily come from Star, and if you ask either of my girls, they'll be the first to tell you they're blood sisters without blinking an eye.

"Are you ready, sweetie?" My wife asks, laying her chin on my shoulder.

"I am. Have you called my brother and Juliana?" Of course, I can't help but laugh as I remember how their two hellions pranked me last week.

"They're all set, as are Felicity and Parker. I'm so glad Shaynah and Blake are able to come, too. It will be a tattoo family party." Star still makes my heart skip a beat. She's like fine wine and only gets better as the years go by. The way she looks at me always ignites a flame inside me.

"It'll be nice to see them all, but I can't wait to get your ass to myself in that room. Whoever had the idea to take turns watching the kids so each couple gets some alone time is a genius. I'm going to ravish you!"

She bites my earlobe before whispering, "You have that backwards. I haven't tasted your sweetness all week because of all this planning."

"You woke me two days ago with your tongue in my pussy," I remind her, and when she gives me that half-grin at me, I instantly get wet.

"Unless you're under me, it's been too long."

"Why must you say things like that when you know we have to go?"

"Are you squirming at the thought of sitting on my face?"

"If you don't quit..." One hand grips the

back of my neck and the other cups my ass, pulling me closer. Her tongue wrestles with mine as the taste of her vanilla coffee hits my senses. She lifts me, so I'm sitting on the counter and moves between my legs. I cry out when she stops our kiss, a knowing glint in her eyes as my breasts rise and fall while I try to draw in air.

"That was unfair and torturous."

"I didn't hear you complain as I was doing it. In fact, I do believe you were seconds from begging me to take you. Wouldn't want to mess up your pristine kitchen, would we?"

"What was the point of getting me all hot and bothered if you weren't going to do anything more than kiss me?"

"I want you drenched when we get to our room," she says with a wink then walks away. "Come on, baby. We don't want to miss the cruise." Oh, she's in trouble now. I plan on being the demanding one tonight, and with the little number I picked up with the help of the girls, she won't be able to resist me. Not that she ever has, whether I'm naked or in ratty pajamas, she's still trying to get at me.

I'm forever lucky that I'm loved by her.

About the Author

Most days you can find Pixie running around trying to juggle 100 hats…one of which is Author. BTW, she still can't believe that's what she gets to call herself that. What started out as a passion for book blogging turned into publishing her very first novella… *Sealed With A Kiss.*

Pixie who is part of the LGBT Community, writes MF, FF and MM stories that are sexy, insta-love stories full of heart and with a HEA.

Her characters not only fall quickly, deeply, but are also possessive in nature. If she's not writing, then she's on Facebook…Tell her to get the hell out of there and get writing.

"Where Love Always Wins."

You can follow Pixie Chica via any of the social media by clicking the link below:
https://linktr.ee/pixiechica

Books by Pixie

Always & Forever Series
Sealed with a Kiss
In Plain Sight

Love Unexpected Series
Love at Sunset
Undeniable Love
Unleashed Love

Valladares Family Saga
Ivy's Rebellion

Tattooed Brides Series
Loved by Her
Loved in the Dark

Lancaster Falls Series
Because of Blue
Because of You

Holiday Hearts
Mistletoe
Undercover Santa
His Christmas Delivery
Stupid Cupid
Altared

Sweetville
Put a Ring on It
Stranded Christmas
Ring of Fire
Good Cop Bad Girl
Happenstance

Latimer Ladies
New Year's Kiss
Sweetness
Last Shot

Price Industries
Mine by Christmas
Give into Temptation

Sizzle Beach
Things We Did Last Summer

Standalones
A Wolfe's Ruby
A Royal Payne
Treat You Better
Teacher's Pet
Playing for Keeps
Curves Rx
My Vampire Mate

Box Sets
Holiday Hearts Collection
The Covingtons
Price Industries

www.ingramcontent.com/pod-product-compliance
Lightning Source LLC
Chambersburg PA
CBHW021039160726

47994CB00006B/2641